THE WOLF
and the
SEVEN LITTLE KIDS

A story by the Brothers Grimm with pictures by Felix Hoffmann

Harcourt, Brace and Company
New York

FOR SUSANNE

Once upon a time there was a mother goat who had seven little kids whom she loved dearly, as all mothers love their children.

One day she had to go into the forest
to fetch some food, so she called her seven little kids
together and said to them:
'My dear children, I must go into the forest.
Beware of the wolf! If you let him in he will eat
you up, every little bit of you.
He often disguises himself, but you will recognize
him straight away because of his hoarse voice and
his black paws.'

The little kids replied:
'Mother dear, we will take care of ourselves, never
fear. You can go away without worrying about us!'

So the mother goat,
       bleating happily, went on her way

It was not long before there was a knocking on the front door and someone called:
'Open the door, my little ones. It is your mother and she has brought something back for each one of you.'

But the little kids could hear that it was the wolf because of his hoarse voice.
'We shan't open the door,' they cried. 'You're not our mother! She has a lovely voice, but yours is hoarse – you are the wolf!'

So the wolf went off
to a grocer's shop and bought a
large piece of chalk and ate it,
to make his voice all smooth.

Then he went back,
knocked at the front door
and called:
'Open the door, my little ones.
It is your mother and she
has brought something back
for each one of you!'

The little kids cried:
'Show us your paw
at the window!'

And when they saw
his black paw,
they cried:
'We shan't open the door.
Our mother doesn't
have black paws –
you are the wolf!'

So the wolf went off to a baker's
and said: 'I've hurt my paws – spread
some dough on them!' And when the baker had spread some dough on his front paws, he ran across to th

aid : 'Sprinkle some white flour on my paws.'

The miller thought : 'This wolf will only cheat me,'
and refused, but the wolf said : 'If you don't,
I'll eat you up !' So the miller was afraid
and made the wolf's front paws white.

Then the wicked wolf went back a third time, knocked on the front door, and called: 'Open the door, my little ones. Your mother has come home and she has brought something for each one of you!'

The little kids cried:
'Show us your paws first so that we can be sure you really are our dear mother.' So he put up his paws to the window,

and when the little kids saw that these
were white, they believed what he said
and opened the door.
Who should come in but

THE WOLF!

The little kids were terrified
and rushed off to hide:

one under the table,
another in the cupboard,
the third on top of the stove,
the fourth under the bench,
the fifth in a corner,
the sixth under the stove.
And the seventh hid inside
　the grandfather clock.

The wolf found them all
and swallowed them
with his great jaws.
The only one he didn't find
was the youngest kid, inside
the grandfather clock.

Then he went out and
lay down under a tree
in the green meadow and
was soon fast asleep.

Not long afterwards mother goat came
back from the forest.

OH DEAR, what a sight met her eyes!

Tables, chairs and benches were overturned,
the milk jug was broken, and the curtain torn.
She looked everywhere for her children
but could not find them.
She called them by name, one after the other,
but there was no answer.
At last, when she got as far as the youngest,
a little voice cried out:
'Mother dearest, I'm inside the grandfather clock.'
Mother goat pulled out the little kid
and he told her how the wolf had come
and eaten up all the others.

You can imagine how she wept for her
poor children!

At long last, in her sorrow, she went outside.

And when she got to the meadow, there was the wolf,
shaking the branches above him with his loud snoring.
Mother goat looked at him from all sides and she saw
that something was stirring and fidgeting inside his
swollen stomach.

'Heavens', she thought, 'is it possible that my poor
children may still be alive?'
So the youngest little kid had to run home to fetch needle and thread and a pair of scissors.

Then mother goat cut open the monster's stomach, and as soon as she had made the first cut, one of the little kids stuck out his head, and as she went on cutting, all six of them jumped out, one after the other, still alive, because in his greed the wolf had swallowed them whole.

What rejoicing there was then!

The little kids hugged their dear mother and started skipping about, but she said to them: 'Now you must go and fetch some stones from the stream so that we can fill the stomach of this wicked animal with them while he is still asleep.'

So the seven little kids hurried off and dragged back some stones from the stream, and stuffed as many as they could into the wolf's stomach.

Then their mother sewed it up
so quickly that the wolf
noticed nothing
and did not even stir.

When the wolf had slept long enough, he got up, and as the stones inside him made him feel terribly thirsty, he wanted to go and drink at the well. But when he started walking, the stones in his stomach scraped and rattled against each other.

So he cried:
'What is it inside my stomach
that rumbles and bumbles and knocks?
I thought it was six little kids,
but it feels like boulders and rocks.'

And when he bent down over the well,
the heavy stones pulled him right into the
water, and he was drowned.

When the seven little kids saw this, t[h]
came running along, shouting:

'THE WOLF IS DEAD!
THE WOLF IS DEAD!'

and, full of joy, they danced with their
mother round and round the well.